House Blessings

ALSO BY JUNE COTNER

Animal Blessings

Baby Blessings

Bedside Prayers

Bless the Beasts

Bless the Day

Christmas Blessings

Family Celebrations

Graces

The Home Design Handbook

Looking for God in All the Right Places

Mothers and Daughters

Wedding Blessings

House Blessings

PRAYERS, POEMS, AND TOASTS CELEBRATING HOME AND FAMILY

June Cotner

CHRONICLE BOOKS

SAN FRANCISCO

Printed in China

Book design by Todd Bates

Library of Congress Control Number: 2004101637
ISBN-10: 0-9748486-0-3
ISBN-13: 978-0-9748486-0-0

House Blessings is produced by becker&mayer!, Bellevue, Washington
www.beckermayer.com

20 19 18 17 16 15 14 13 12 11

CHRONICLE BOOKS
680 SECOND STREET
SAN FRANCISCO, CA 94107
WWW.CHRONICLEBOOKS.COM

Dedication

House Blessings is dedicated
with love and affection
to my dear friend
and exceptional artist and author
Jody Houghton,
who gave me the idea for this book!

Home is a landscape etched on your heart.

Jody Houghton

Contents

3. Our Children

4. Our Garden

5. Graces & Toasts

6. Holidays & Celebrations

7. Reflections

Letter to Readers

Who can resist an invitation to dwell in the comforts and pleasures of a home well loved? Who among us can't appreciate images of loved ones waiting just behind the door, eager to assemble after returning from the challenges of our daily lives? Or the idea of comfortable conversation and a lovingly prepared meal—providing physical and emotional nourishment—in a familiar, peaceful setting where we can truly be ourselves?

Our homes—the dressing rooms for the stage of life—are so integral to our well-being they are often overlooked when we count our blessings. But to rediscover this elusive gratitude, one needs merely to think of a soldier in the field who longs to return to his country, or a commuter stuck in traffic trying to get home for dinner, or, of course, the unfortunate who has never known the ordinary comforts of a place called "home."

I have my own unique relationship with the concept of home. Some years ago, before my love of books became my main passion, I worked in the field of architecture. In fact, my first book, *The Home Design Handbook*, was about the subject! But obviously a "home" is more than the structure we live in. A home is an intimate physical space that spiritually connects those who dwell within it. Blessing this space is a natural human inclination, as evidenced through the wealth of blessings and rituals spanning cultures and religious traditions.

My own home-based traditions and deep love of home and family compelled me to assemble this collection. The idea of a book to honor the simple pleasures of home was seeded by my good friend and gift-creating guru Jody Houghton. She suggested a volume devoted to this universal idea would be an appropriate addition to my collections of verse. She was right.

The idea was instantly fueled by thoughtful submissions from contributors who shared sentiments that were both personal and all embracing. The resulting treasure trove of wisdoms and insights, coupled with traditional sayings and blessings for the home and family, have blended into an enchanting collection that, like a happy home, is a delight to share.

So I invite you, dear readers, to bring this collection into your homes and hearts and be warmed by the blessings, meditations, prayers, and poems herein that celebrate and honor that sacred space we call home.

Thanks

My biggest thanks to Jim Becker and Andy Mayer at becker&mayer!, one of the largest book producing and packaging companies in the country, for all the generous help you've given me in overseeing the publication of *House Blessings*. I love the creativity and innovation you both bring to all your projects.

As always, my sincere appreciation to Denise Marcil for all the support you've given me over the years.

A special thanks to Anna Johnson at becker&mayer!, who oversaw the development of *House Blessings* and sold the book to special sales accounts. I greatly enjoy working with you and value our friendship, which formed as a result. In the course of creating *House Blessings*, I had the good fortune to work with the following people at becker&mayer!: Adrienne Wiley (who coordinated all editorial work), Todd Bates (who designed the fabulous cover and interior), and Leah Finger and Sheila Kamuda (who coordinated the production).

Deep gratitude goes to the incredible poets who have contributed to my books for over a decade now. I've had the pleasure of meeting more than fifty of you in the course of my travels around the country. Even among those of you I have not yet met, many of you feel like good friends. I greatly appreciate your enthusiasm and our feeling of partnership. I truly want to find a vehicle for your fine words. I feel we're a team—you create the wonderful words of inspiration and comfort, and I try to find the best book for them.

I owe much thanks to my dear daughter, Kirsten Casey, who helps my business in countless ways. You're a fine editor, highly creative, very efficient, and a perfect business partner! Also, thanks to my musician son, Kyle Myrvang. Your fast fingers on the piano translate to a fast typing speed—thanks for giving me such a quick turnaround on the selections for *House Blessings*! I also greatly appreciate the excellent insight and creative talent Rebecca Carter brought to this book.

I'm profoundly grateful to Jim Graves, my dear husband, who supports me with endless encouragement and practical household chores. We love our home life, and Jim makes it possible for me to have both a cozy, loving home and a very satisfying business life. I'm so thankful for all of the home-cooked meals you've lovingly prepared and all the big and little chores you do to make our house truly a home.

And last, I'm grateful to God for guiding me on my path of creating books that inspire, encourage, and comfort others as we navigate the roads of our lives. I feel very blessed.

Our Home

May Blessings Be Upon Your Home

May blessings be upon your home,
 Your roof and hearth and walls;
May there be lights to welcome you
 When evening's shadow falls—
The love that like a guiding star
 Still signals when you roam;
A book, a friend—these be the things
 That make a house a home.

Myrtle Reed

A Home Is Built with Peace and Love

A home is built with peace and love,
and not of wood or stone,
a place where happiness lives,
and memories are sown.

Author unknown

An Irish Blessing

May you always be blessed
with walls for the wind,
a roof for the rain,
a warm cup of tea by the fire,
laughter to cheer you,
those you love near you,
and all that your heart might desire.

Author unknown

Crossing the Threshold

Crossing the threshold to enter the world
take security and love, mortar of this home,
as your foundation today
Let every thought, word, and action
come from such a place of peace

Upon your return
release worry, fear, or anger
that may have arisen while away
Breathe deep the familiar fragrance
of sanctuary; wash your eyes
with the colors and sights that signal
safe deliverance, once again,
home

Arlene Gay Levine

Our Home

No Matter What Happens

No matter what happens
In the rush of daily life,
May your home welcome you at day's end
With comfort, peace, and light.
May it be your shelter
Throughout any hardships,
And may you know many blessings
In the company of loved ones and true friends.

Corrine De Winter

Our Home

Housewarming Blessing

(Present this blessing with a large container of salt and a loaf of bread.)

Accept this gift of salt and bread
with a blessing for your new place:

May harmony
grace your home
long after every grain
of this salt is gone.

May bread be plentiful
and nourish those
gathered at your table.

Mary Kolada Scott

Our Home

House Blessing

Your house is Love's house.
It is a sanctuary, a garden,
a safe haven.
May it be delightful.
May it be a home that encourages
creativity and peace,
togetherness and private time.
May it be an environment
that celebrates life, untidy and ever flowing.
May simplicity be honored in your house,
valuing love above all else.
May daily chores and small moments
all be approached with reverence and with love.

Our Home

Mistakes may be seen as lessons learned.
Kindness, forgiveness, laughter, joy,
and calm enthusiasm
will nourish all who enter through its doors.
May all who visit leave refreshed.
May all who live in your house
live in contentment and harmony,
dreaming beautiful dreams,
rejoicing in the way things are.

Ingrid Goff-Maidoff

Our Home

More Than Bricks and Wood

More than bricks and wood,
our house is made of memories.
More than doors and windows,
our house holds good times shared.
More than rooms and furnishings,
our home is filled with love.

Nancy Priff

Blessing for a New House

Blessed be this house
& all who dwell within.

May you eat well,
drink to surfeit,

make love
& make merry,

lie down in content
& rise up again in joy.

May peace attend
your comings & goings.

May happiness wait on you,
& upon this new hearth

every day
may the kettle sing.

Marjorie Rommel

Our Home

Aromatic Memories

Fill your home with pleasant smells
Aromas to remember
Baking bread, lavender baths,
Fresh ground coffee, cinnamon candles
Each takes its place in family folklore
Tucked away in nostalgic drawers
For a day when the sky is gray
And you sit alone
Longing for the company of family
Hundreds of miles away
That warm, spicy, pungent vapor
Will escape from its closet
And invade your senses
When you need it the most
Wrapping you once more
In the comfort of familiarity

Gwyneth M. Bledsoe

Our Home

A Ritual for Moving

Starting at the front door of your "old" home, light incense or a jar candle, or carry a live plant or other special object and say: "Bless this doorway, through which love and friendship have come to us. We remember the stories of our lives, which entered here and filled our hearts and this home. We are here to celebrate and to gather our memories of this place we have called home for _____ years."

As family members stand in a circle in each space, invite everyone to share a memory that took place there, concluding with, "I am grateful for this place." Then, after everyone has spoken say, "We leave this space giving thanks and carrying these memories with us." Do this through the back and front yards, concluding where you began, at the front door, repeating the phrase a final time, in unison.

At your new home, place the object you carried through your old home in the entrance of your new home and say, "The memories we bring with us and the moments yet to be are what connect us to each other and make us a family. Blessed be."

The Reverend J. Lynn James

Farewell to Our Home

We have to say good-bye now;
we're moving out, moving on,
but not before walking once more
through rooms now echoing with silence—
polished floors bare of rugs and toys,
closets emptied of racquets and parkas.
Here the bedrooms of studies, love, and dreams,
the family room where videos thundered,
the kitchen where soup simmered as cookies
puffed with promise in backlit ovens.
There the windows where once we waited
for children exploding in joyful release
from carpools and school buses, and, later,
a homecoming husband already smiling
in anticipation of welcome and respite.
Stepping outside we touch trees' rough bark,
push the swing, hear in memory a gleeful,
"Higher, Mommy, higher now."

Our Home

Sitting for a moment on the lawn, we
remember the pets sun-napping right here . . .
But it's time to go. Placing a letter of welcome
on the kitchen counter for the new family,
we close the door behind us, whisper,
"Thanks, dear home, for all our memories."

SuzAnne C. Cole

Our Home

Housewarming

We hope you'll find pleasure,
friends and family,
as you gather here today
to warm our new home.

Within these walls may peace dwell,
cheerfulness abound;
for a house filled with loved ones
is what makes a home.

So come often, friends, family—
welcome mat is out.
Come sit with us by the fire,
make yourself at home.

Judy Barnes

Our Home

Moving-In-Day Prayer

Let the sound
of laughter
Brighten each corner
of this house
And the strength
of prayer
Lay at the foundation
of your dreams.

Marilyn Huntman Giese

Home Song

Your new, yet seasoned, house says welcome.
It asks you to look around—and listen
to voices that build its tradition.

Picture a bride once carried over the threshold.
Imagine small, mittened hands making a snowman.
Wonder at trinkets appearing in unlikely places.
Hear laughter and songs from holidays and parties.

Now add your joys, your life, to the blend.

Joanne Keaton

Our Home

Hand and Hand—Heart to Heart

We set up a household.
Hand and hand—
Heart to heart—

Speaking and smiling,
We made a house a home—
Seeking spaces and places
For all that was packed and boxed.

Shifting and arranging,
We set in place
Bountiful housewares
And beautiful gifts.

Ordering and sorting,
We made sacred space for God's grace,
So this new home would forever embrace
The love that is shared within it.

Annie Dougherty

Our Home

On Entering a New Home

It may be cabin, villa, mansion,
Palace, castle, or cottage;
A house is a sanctuary
Offering safe refuge.
Warm and cozy,
Light and airy.
A homestead and a household,
A nest to rear the young,
An interior to grow old in
And a perch where songs are sung.
A residence for laughter
Or tears of joy and sorrows,
Keeper of past memories
And path to our tomorrows.
May these walls and floors
and rooftop dome
Turn this humble house into
A gracious, love-filled home.

Sheila Forsyth

Our Home

Mountain Retreat

I come to you for rest,
for retreat.
Leaving behind
noise of responsibility,
cacophony of worry,
walking away
from cluttered life,
I seek your simple ways.

I come to you for thought,
for dreams.
Your fresh air
feeds my hopes.

Wrapped in a quilt
of mountain green,
you enfold me with life.
You sing lullabies
to rhythms of a passing stream.

You give me rest.

Julia Taylor Ebel

Our Home

Cabin Prayer

Let this be our quiet place,
    Our small haven from the noise and bustle of everyday.
Let us find within these walls
    The joy of family togetherness
    As well as individual moments
    Of reflection, clarity, and inspiration
    To rejuvenate our souls.
Let us cherish the beauty of the natural world beyond our doorstep,
    Respect and delight in the creatures
    Which will be our new neighbors.
And let the memories we create here,
    The peace we find here,
    Give us heart's ease whenever we're far
    From our cabin home.

Sharon Hudnell

Our Home

Bless This Beloved Old Farmhouse

This house has been home to all manner of things,
To creatures with tails and with feathers and wings.
Up high in the attic, or deep in the cellar,
How safe and secure is each little dweller
With nests in the attic, the chimney and floors,
Up under the beams and perched over the doors,
Evading the traps and all things that swat,
Residing herein, whether wanted or not.

Occasional reminders of those gone before
In creaking old floorboards and soft-closing doors,
The chiming of clocks that have not worked in years
By spirits unseen who are lingering here.
Two centuries of life have been shared in this place
But those who've departed leave always a trace.
No matter who lives in this stately old home,
There isn't a chance that they'll be here alone.

Our Home

Now here will I welcome my family and friends.
Be at home in this house, whosoever comes in
To share with me laughter and music and tears,
And don't mind the others who're living in here.
It's weathered and drafty, but solid and true.
Today it's my home, but I'm just passing through.
Please bless this old house, oh my dear Lord, I pray,
So the next generation can love it someday.

Sandra E. McBride

Our Home

An RV Blessing

This is a wish for the freedom you desire;
for the caress of a Chinook breeze in the winter,
a shady resting spot in the summer,
an autumn quilt to wrap up in:
the sea-blue field of flax on the prairie,
crimson blooms in a desert garden,
bordered by the white down of snowgeese
as they return home in the spring.

And when there are seasonal storms,
we know they'll bring new friends inside,
in from inclement weather,
for a serving of your gracious hospitality:
laughter, love, and a hearty
"Welcome to our Traveling Home."

Carol L. MacKay

Our Home

25

Blessing for a Retirement Home

Dear God,

_____ & _____ have lived in more than one home during the span of their lives. Each of those homes holds its own special share of memories. Today, we join them to begin a new tradition of memories in this retirement home. Bless the latter portion of their lives even more than you did the first.

Sandra Holmes McGarrity

Our Home

Bless This House — A Texas Prayer

Let us pray.
Bless this house, oh Lord, we cry.
Please keep it cool in mid-July.
Bless the walls where termites dine,
while ants and roaches march in time.
Bless our yard where spiders pass
fireant castles in the grass.
Bless the garage, a home to please
carpenter beetles, ticks, and fleas.
Bless the love bugs, two by two,
the gnats and mosquitoes that feed on you.
Millions of creatures that fly or crawl,
In Texas, Lord, you've put them all!!
But this is home, and here we'll stay,
So thank you, Lord, for insect spray!

Author unknown

Our Home

Our Hands Were Moved

We had asked for peace,
Universe offered bliss.

Our hands were moved
to join together,
our imaginations summoned
to envision our lives.

Grateful, we thank life
and the wisdom of Spirit.

The days increase
and our home is built
from the breath of our hearts
and our souls' fire.

In wonder we witness
a miracle rising in love.

Kate Robinson

Our Home

Blessing for a Jewish Home

May this *Mezuzah**,
Filled with the words of God
And fixed upon the doorpost,
Remind us daily
Who we are as we enter
And who we remain as we leave.
May it be a sign to all
That our home is a harbor,
Secure and sacred,
Founded with faith
And bound up with love.

*A small box, affixed to the doorposts of a Jewish home,
containing the handwritten first paragraph of a Jewish
prayer called the *She'ma*.

Our Home

29

May the walls echo
With laughter,
And the halls
Listen patiently to Life's calls.
Though winds may blow
And rain rage upon the roof,
May this home weather every storm
And always be
Welcoming and warm.

Andria W. Rosenbaum

Our Home

Live Well Within Your New Home

As you step across the threshold
Take measurements in your mind
For this is where you will live, love, eat
Cherish each moment within these walls

Breathe beauty, art, and love into this place
Let forgiveness and grace have their way
Hang garlands of mercy from the porch
Your light will shine bright to strangers

Gwyneth M. Bledsoe

Our Home

A Prayer for Our Home

Dear Lord,
May the walls
of our home
always know
the joy of laughter,
the beauty of friendships,
and the soft, golden glow
of hearts united in love.

Cindy Chuksudoon

Within the Four Walls

I think that the most significant work we ever do, in our whole world, in our whole life, is done within the four walls of our own home.

Stephen R. Covey

A Traditional Welsh Blessing

May its windows catch the sun
and its doors be open wide
to friends and loved ones.

May each room resound with laughter
and may the walls shut out troubles
and hold in warmth and cheer.

May this house be filled
with joy in the morning
and sweet dreams at night.

May it be a home
where love has come to live.

Author unknown

Our Home

We Pray This House

We pray that each room in this house
will resound with the sounds of laughter and joyfulness,
that its sturdy structure
will shelter us from the elements
and be a refuge of peace from the trials of daily life.
We pray this house will become a beloved home
for all who live within its walls
and that constant faith and hopeful dreams
will always be a part of its foundation.

Corrine De Winter

Our Home

Family Home

Home is a place where we can be silent
and still be heard . . .
Where we can ask and find out
who we are . . .
Where sorrow is divided and joy multiplied . . .
Where we share and love
and grow.

Author unknown

2

Family & Friends

Hearts at Home

May the heart of our home
always be a safe haven
where we can gather together
in good times and bad
to enjoy the unity, strength,
and support of family . . .
And may we always be thankful
for the warm comforts of kinship
and find our soul's greatest delight
in the most precious gift of our love.

Cindy Chuksudoon

The Joy of Belonging

May God give you
the peace of stability,
the joy of belonging,
and
the comfort of family and friends
in your new nesting place.

Malinda Fillingim

Family & Friends

Our Hearts

Dearest God,
Wherever our hearts choose to call home,
with Your love and Your grace,
keep this family unshakable . . .
with our love for each other,
keep this family unbreakable . . .

Anne Calodich Fone

Family & Friends

An Irish House Blessing

May the roof above us never fall in
and may the friends gathered below it never fall out.

Author unknown

Home Rules

If you sleep on it . . . make it up.
If you wear it . . . hang it up.
If you drop it . . . pick it up.
If you eat out of it . . . put it in the sink.
If you step in it . . . wipe it off.
If you open it . . . close it.
If you empty it . . . fill it up.
If it rings . . . answer it.
If it howls . . . feed it.
If it cries . . . love it.

Author unknown

Family & Friends

More Than a House

It's a place to raise your family,
And a place to laugh with friends.
It's a place to put your feet up,
And rest at the work day's end.
With space to store your treasures,
And space to make your own,
It's a place to play,
It's a place to love,
It's the place that you call home.

Andrea L. Mack

In Appreciation of the Family Pet

They love without strings attached, these loving beasts of your hand, O God of amazing critters. Bless them, for they bless us even when they leave muddy pawprints on clean floors, ignore our commands, and shed on the furniture. Keep us worthy of their trust.

Margaret Anne Huffman
(1941–2000)

Forgiveness

Gentle God,
grant that at home
where we are most truly ourselves,
where we are known at our best and worst,
we may learn to forgive and be forgiven.

A New Zealand Prayer Book

Family & Friends

May You Be Blessed

Whether you come in to visit
or just to rest
when you enter our home
may you be blessed.

Author unknown

3

Our Children

Our Children Are Like Seeds

Our children are like seeds,
   given to us in unmarked envelopes.
We sprinkle them with love
   and daily let them shine in the sun.
Their roots are well grounded,
   and their shoots are many.
We do not yet know when they will bloom
   Or what their flowers will be.

Rebecca K. Wyss

Our Children

The Enlargement of Time

What parents save—spelling tests in pencil,
paper lanterns, a drawing of a house.
Beneath a border of blue, spokes of sun
shine onto four grinning stick figures,
who stand on a slice of lawn,
forked fingers linked to those nearby.
Childhood becomes sacred
the moment we turn our heads.

Linda Goodman Robiner

Our Children

Paradise

The shouts and screams of laughter,
the toys spilled in the hall;
I pick up shoes and jackets
and put away a doll.
Cookie crumbs seem never-ending,
clothes lay everywhere,
Quiet is a funny word—
In fact, it's rather rare.
Only when at night they sleep
are my children calm and still,
Yet I yearn for noise and racket;
It makes my life fulfilled.
Others call it an annoyance,
"Absurd!" they say it is,
But I call my home Paradise,
And I owe it all to kids.

Jennifer Lynn Clay
(Age 13, reflecting how her mother feels)

Our Children

54

A Child's Sandcastle

He builds it with faith,
creates it with love,
makes it the way he
wants it to be.
Don't change it to fit
your image,
otherwise it is no longer
the child's sandcastle.

Paula Timpson

The Best Way

The best way to keep kids at home is to make the home a pleasant atmosphere.

Author unknown

Now and Then

Now when I hear you at night,
I awaken.
But then,
I rose to nurture you,
to feel your tiny being,
and to savor your softness.

Now when you wear my shoes,
they fit.
But then,
when you played dress-up,
they dwarfed your tiny feet
and made you sweetly silly.

Now when you ask me questions,
I ponder.

But then,
when curiosity was simple,
it was easy to answer
and watch your wonderment grow.

Now when I watch you maturing,
I remember.
But then,
when looking ahead was all,
I wondered who you would be
and waited for you to become.

Tell me.
How did Then
get to be Now
So quickly?

Elayne Clift

Our Children

58

On Leaving My Special Place

I'll not leave for college
for six months;
already, they're planning
what to do with my room.

Mother wants
to make it the "office,"
with the computer
and a guest bed
for Grandma and Grandpa
when they visit.

My brother wants the room,
though I can't think why;
his room is bigger.

Our Children

When I come home,
will I have a place?
Will I be the "guest"?

Bless this room,
my dolls,
my books,
my cat,
and my memories.

Shirley Nelson

Our Children

To My Children

The day you were born
The whole world sang.

The bells, touched with gladness,
Incessantly rang.

The forest was bathed in the
Sunset's soft glow,

In joy you were blessed
To live and to grow.

Gwen Tremain Runyard

My Mother's Prayers

I remember my mother's prayers and they have always followed me.
They have clung to me all my life.

Abraham Lincoln
(1809–1865)

Our Children

Little Souls

Each morning brings me happiness
because of these little souls
always balancing their charm on my heart.

Each has angel wings that embrace me with love
and meets my affection equally with their devotion.

Everything in my life is multiplied.
The love and magic.
The grace and laughter.
The beauty.

For these little souls I cast my dreams to the wind
so that their wings will always carry me with them.
Their souls forever one with mine.

Lori Eberhardy

Our Children

Family Conversation

I think a child is particularly fortunate if he grows up in a family
where his imagination can be fed . . . I think it is a tremendous loss
to a child to grow up in a family without conversation. There should
be discussions of ideas, of the fantastic things that are happening all
over the world, the new discoveries in science and archaeology, of
local or distant problems and their possible solutions.

Eleanor Roosevelt
(1884—1962)

Our Children

Memories

These are my favorite childhood memories:

Baking cookies with my mom, watching Saturday morning cartoons, dressing up my cat in doll clothes, building forts in the living room, singing with my Dad, and playing baseball with my brother so he would play dolls with me.

My childhood memories are not complex. Just happy times spent enjoying the company of those who meant the most to me—my family.

Mary Katherine Devine

Letting Go

I've brought you to the mountain . . .
The climb is yours.

I've brought you to the shore . . .
The sea is yours.

I've brought you to the sky . . .
The wings are yours.

I've brought you through the shadows . . .
The light is yours.

I've brought you to this day . . .
Tomorrow is yours.

Sandra E. McBride

Our Children

4

Our Garden

Somewhere in Every Garden

Somewhere in every garden, there must be at least one spot, a quiet garden seat, in which a person—or two people—can reach into themselves and be in touch with nothing else but nature.

Christopher Alexander

Night Blooming Garden

Following the evening's intoxicating breeze
wandering down the winding path
lying within the shadows
of the night blooming garden
Moonflowers, climbing the fence in disarray
Evening Primrose, tickling senses gently
Tracing the wonderful spicy scent
of the evening-scented stock
Sitting down on an inviting bench
closing my eyes, breathing deeply
inhaling the delicate mixture of scents
I relax, unwinding from the day's stress
quietly letting nature perform her magic

Linda Lee Ruzicka

Turning the Garden Under,

as the hoe whispers erase, erase,
and last year's neat rows disappear,
the final editing.
Unlike paper, the ground forgives,
eager to begin again, fill up with green.
The garden accepts whatever is sown:
scratch out carrots, they appear.
Imagine pumpkins, heavy and fat
as summer storms, and, surprised
as Cinderella, you find them in August.
Nothing is as clean as dirt.

Barbara Crooker

Bless This Garden

This garden echoes
with children laughing,
eating raspberries,
playing with the puppy.

Arranging plantings,
I smell the rich earth;
I see the parties
held in this blessed space.

The roses bloom,
the birds come to feed,
the cat slips through the fence.

A quiet, peaceful spot,
alive with memories.
A growing place,
for fruit, vegetables,
flowers, animals,
children, love.

Shirley Nelson

Our Garden

Old Hoer's Prayer

May the weeds wilt before you; may the vegetables rise up to feed you; and may the bugs stay always on the other side of the fence.

Kathryn E. Mason

My Garden in a Box

For some, their gardens grace acres,
rolling down hills, tripping along meadows,
flowers rising up like colorful flags,
waving as they beckon you to them.
But mine is confined (rather succinctly)
to wooden boundaries that fit a shelf
above my kitchen sink.

There it sits, an abridged arboretum,
surrounded by Lilliputian Redwood borders,
fencing beauty within while keeping
insects and soapsuds without.

Though its size may be small,
quality is not measured in volume,
and the subtle bouquet of lavender,
commingled with detergent, floods
my senses and this gardener's heart.

Susan Rogers Norton

In a Garden

In your strong soil,
I plant seeds of dreams—
beans, tomatoes, squash.

With patience I water.
I hoe with hope,
weed out doubts,
imagine green, yellow, red.

In company of sun,
whispering wind,
and robins' free song,
I tend a hallowed place in my soul.

Our Garden

And when harvest comes,
you give me more than baskets full.
From your soil
I gather strength.

I touch life on your vines.
I taste your fruit
and know that I hold seeds
to bring forth life.

Julia Taylor Ebel

Our Garden

I Walk With You

I walk out in my garden
with You in quiet prayer.
Starlings sing a requiem
assuring me You're there.

Clover mixed with violets
stretch their necks to see
the face of Heaven's sunrise
walking close to me.

A bud of green protruding
from a barren tree
proves how Your forgiveness
sets my spirit free.

Thank You for walking
each day by my side,
listening to all the prayers
my heart still holds inside.

Mary Lenore Quigley

The Garden Year

January brings the snow,
Makes our feet and fingers glow.

February brings the rain,
Thaws the frozen lake again.

March brings breezes, loud and shrill,
To stir the dancing daffodil.

April brings the primrose sweet,
Scatters daisies at our feet.

May brings flocks of pretty lambs
Skipping by their fleecy dams.

June brings tulips, lilies, roses,
Fills the children's hands with posies.

Hot July brings cooling showers,
Apricots, and gillyflowers.

August brings the sheaves of corn,
Then the harvest home is borne.

Warm September brings the fruit;
Sportsmen then begin to shoot.

Fresh October brings the pheasant;
Then to gather nuts is pleasant.

Dull November brings the blast;
Then the leaves are whirling fast.

Chill December brings the sleet,
Blazing fire, and Christmas treat.

Sara Coleridge
(1802–1852)

Our Garden

Morning's Gift

Like a Pied Piper
the sounds of early morning
coax me out of bed,
and I follow
knowing that the morning
holds secrets
the rest of the day will never know.

As I approach the garden
veiled in fog
it appears unfamiliar.
Rows of bush beans and staked tomatoes
Stand like strange ghosts in another world.
I enter that misty island
and I, too, am in another world
hidden from the cares of the day at hand.
I kneel
to harvest lettuce and new potatoes.
My soul is nourished for the day's journey.

Molly Srode

All Week Long, the Irises Have Unfolded,

shaping the air with their colored wings.
Their song is invisible; they speak in tongues
as along each stalk, they break out in flight.
They cannot bear their beauty, but arc to earth
as I come by to cut them free.
I wrap the blooms in thinnest tissue,
present them to a neighbor,
and her face breaks out in petals
and her eyes are full of sky.

Barbara Crooker

Our Garden

A Garden Blessing

The kiss of the sun for pardon,
  The song of the birds for mirth—
One is nearer God's heart in a garden
  Than anywhere else on earth.

Dorothy Frances Gurney
(1858–1932)

5

Graces & Toasts

A Toast

Here's to *years* of happiness,
and *months* of sunny skies,
to *weeks* of reaching mountain peaks,
and *days* of caring eyes,
to *hours* of hope and tenderness,
and *minutes* of delight,
On *second* thought, we wish you love
on this, your special night.

Carol Murray

A Grace for Our World

For food in a world where many walk in hunger;
For faith in a world where many walk in fear;
For friends in a world where many walk alone;
We give you thanks, O Lord. Amen.

Anglican Church of Canada

A Ceremony of the Ordinary

We say no prayer, though perhaps we should. But in a quiet way, the table itself is prayer enough. It draws us into a circle, the most mythic and powerful of all human shapes. We pass the food from hand to hand, the most sacramental of all common human acts. Though it remains unspoken, even unrealized, our shared meal creates a bond among us, and, for a moment, makes us one.

Kent Nerburn

Gratitude

Give thanks unto the Lord,
We offer now our praise,
For bounties never ceasing
And goodness, all our days.

We gather round this table,
Our fellowship so sweet,
As kindred hearts together,
In celebration, meet.

Norma Woodbridge

A Morning Grace for Family

With vigor, awe, and great expectation, we greet You this morning, O God of dawn and rising dew. Go with us into our busy day, holding each one in the palm of your hand; nudge us toward creative responses and inspired actions in all we do and say and return us to the family circle full of tales to tell, questions to share. And now in gratitude, we look back to everything that was good yesterday, and, in faith and hope, face forward, ready for today.

Margaret Anne Huffman
(1941–2000)

Irish Grace

May this food restore our strength, giving new energy to tired limbs, new thoughts to weary minds. May this drink restore our soul, giving new vision to dry spirits, new warmth to cold hearts. And once refreshed, may we give new pleasure to You, who gives us all.

Author unknown

We Give Thanks

We give thanks to the Power that makes for Meeting,
for our table has been a place of dialogue and friendship.
We give thanks to Life.
May we never lose touch with the simple joy and wonder
of sharing a meal.

Rabbi Rami M. Shapiro

An Evening Grace

Under the roof that shelters us
from wind and rain
We are thankful
we have a safe place to return to
When the day is over and dreams come again.
Let us always remember
those who are without a warm space,
Those who are tired and alone,
and let us know how fortunate we are
To call these rooms our Home.

Corrine De Winter

We Give Thanks through the Seasons

We give thanks for daffodils,
for butterflies and fragrant hills,
for spring's new gifts that bring us joy—
We give thanks, each girl and boy.

We give thanks for fireflies,
for hummingbirds and starlit skies,
for summer's bounty, big and small—
We give thanks for one and all.

We give thanks for crunching leaves
for football games and longer sleeves,
for harvest moon and candy corn—
We give thanks this autumn morn.

We give thanks for Santa's elves,
for shopping trips and jingle bells,
for twinkling lights and manger hay—
We give thanks on Christmas day.

Dena Dyer

Graces & Toasts

Prayer of Gratitude

God, I am thankful for the people to whom I can relate in all situations.
I am grateful for all of them—
for those called "family" who provide community,
for those called "leaders" who give guidance,
for those called "enemies" who help me see my faults,
for those called "colleagues" who share responsibilities,
for those called "scholars" who teach important lessons,
for those called "helpers" who enable us to be of help,
for those called "comforters" who dry my tears, unafraid of my weeping.

Author unknown

Graces & Toasts

Prayer in Community

We sing a song of gladness
As we celebrate this day,
With festive hearts and thankfulness
For this food, we pray.

We thank You, Lord, for plenty,
For Your mercy and Your grace,
And for each one gathered 'round,
May Your tenderness embrace.

Norma Woodbridge

May Life Protect Us

May life protect us and surprise us
And be no more harsh than our spirits may bear.
Amen.

Congregation of Abraxas (adapted)

Chinese Blessing

Round the table
Peace and joy prevail.
May all who share
This season's delight
Enjoy countless more.

Author unknown

Eskimo Toast

May you have warmth in your igloo,
oil in your lamp,
and peace in your heart.

Author unknown

A Friendship Toast

To your good health, old friend,
may you live for a thousand years,
and I be there to count them.

> *Robert Smith Surtees*
> *(1803–1864)*

Mennonite Blessing

Thank you for the wind, rain,
and sun and pleasant weather,
thank you for this our food
and that we are together.

Author unknown

6

Holidays & Celebrations

To Life

Enjoy.
Breathe deep.
Dance a little,
if only in your heart.
Drink to the future
but savor the past.
Sing an old song.
Say a blessing.
Celebrate.

Joanne Seltzer

For Our Anniversary

I look inside my heart, and I always find you there.
Your devotion is unfailing, your love overflowing.

When I need to be loved unconditionally
and treated with tenderness,
you surprise me with a love more wonderful
than I could ever imagine
and sweeter than any star within my reach.

When I am searching for an answer to my prayers,
when I need forgiveness and a taste of grace,
each day I am gently reminded of your healing touch.

So as I reflect on all the blessings that life can bring,
I am most comforted by the promise that
beyond this moment
our love will always endure.

Lori Eberhardy

In Celebration of a Newborn

Baby dear,
your sails are set
for the joyous trip
called life.
May you always find
brisk winds,
a guiding star,
and safe harbors.

Barbara J. Holt

Happy Birthday to You

The view from the summit of your birthday is awesome! So much yet to do, so many sights to see, spread before you like paths through an evergreen valley. What joy to be given another happy return on the day of your birth. Make each day count, each choice creative. At the turnstile of this new year, excited and ready, the candles on your cake beckon light forward to the party you call life.

Margaret Anne Huffman
(1941–2000)

Today Is Yours

Today is yours—
       to reflect on your dreams.
       to reach for the future.
       to savour your individuality
       and dance to your own rhythm.
A day to celebrate yourself,
Happy birthday.

Andrea L. Mack

Family Reunion Grace

We arrived today, God of then and now, as near strangers, for families no longer live close by. Be with us as we meet around our common root to rededicate our ancestors' memories. Be with us as we take our places *as* ancestors for the young ones; help us be worthy of remembrance by generations to come. Through this time of catching up, embrace and return us to our distant homes renewed, refreshed, and revitalized until we again join hands with You around this family table.

Margaret Anne Huffman
(1941–2000)

Thanksgiving Grace

We gather around this feasting table, humbled by our bounty, oh Lord of abundant life, in the face of how much more we have before us than we need. Thank you that we have the luxury of overeating; help us learn to share not only our food, but also our lives so that others may, on next Thanksgiving Day, have reason to pause, give thanks, and pass on what has been given to them. Help us also learn better how to live as grateful children . . . delighted, surprised, and generous with the sharing of our good fortune. And now join us in our home amidst food, friends, family, as we each name silently that for which we give the greatest thanks.

Margaret Anne Huffman
(1941–2000)

Each Chanukah Candle

As we light each Chanukah candle,
And watch our children's faces,
We pray for understanding
Among people of all races.

Jill Williams

Christmas Eve Grace

A holly wreath upon the door.
A fire burning bright.
A boldly shining silver star.
The gift of heavenly light.

Tinsel frosted Christmas trees.
Angelic choirs sing,
Hymns of joy and restful peace,
This blessed night shall bring.

Louise I. Webster

Christmas Past

The memories most endearing
No matter where we roam
Are those of Christmas Past
In a place we knew as home.

The magic of the season
With scent of wax and pine,
The aroma from the kitchen
That beckoned us to dine.

The dancing lights upon the tree
That cast their Yuletide spell,
The joyous song of carolers—
Peace on Earth—Noel!

The ghosts of cherished loved ones;
They live and always will,
For no one ever dies in
The place where time stands still.

The treasured scenes of yesteryear—
Could prayers but make them last;
Traditions of the heart live on
In dreams of Christmas Past.

C. David Hay

A Blessing for the New Year

God, bless our year
giving us
time for the task
peace for the pathway
wisdom for the work
friends for the fireside
love to the last.

The Mothers Union Anthology of Public Prayers

7

Reflections

You Can Be You

Making a house work for you, getting it to deliver the emotional rewards—love, personal expression, and a sense of well-being—requires knowing yourself and knowing how you'd like to live. Your house is that special place where you can be you.

JoAnn Barwick

Reflections

Character

It is difficult to understand
anybody without visiting his home.
Houses reveal character.

Gilbert Highet
(1906–1978)

Heart-Light

May the light be always on
wherever home may be
and our hearts forever lit with love
by each sweet memory.

Anne Calodich Fone

Reflections

A Feeling of Home

Home is a feeling . . .
of peace, comfort, and satisfaction.
A sanctuary to rest, heal, and refresh,
Knowing this is where I belong.

Mary Huff Chandler

Reflections

Through Wisdom a House Is Built

Through wisdom a house is built,
And by understanding it is established;
By knowledge the rooms are filled
With all precious and pleasant riches.

Proverbs 24:3–4, NKJV

Reflections

My Kitchen

My kitchen is a mystical place. It is a place where the sounds and the odors carry meaning that transfers from the past and bridges into the future.

Pearl Bailey

My Grandmother's Kitchen

When I think of my grandmother's kitchen, I am surrounded by white. White wooden cupboards with hutch tops and a roll-top bread box; pearl-white, slightly chipped porcelain counters; ivory wallpaper spritzed with a frosted pattern; bleached linoleum faded from the sun; a massive kitchen table covered with chalky oil cloth and perched on thick white legs—much like her own that were always covered with beige lisle stockings rolled down below the kneecap with strangulating garters.

My grandmother dusted the kitchen with a haze of flour as she scooped up handfuls for piecrusts, noodles, dumplings—the only measuring tool her cupped fingers.

The light oak icebox held local farm eggs and sturdy glass bottles of milk with an inch of cream at the neck. The wood stove hummed with broth boiling. The propane oven vented aromas of yeast rising, apple slices bubbling with cinnamon. When days are dim or times darken, I float back to that white kitchen, feel cool porcelain, hear Irish songs lifting, imagine floury hands and thick cotton stockings.

Donna Wahlert

Reflections

124

The Infinity of Housework

No matter how often I vacuum,
Dust bunnies play tag in the corners within the hour.

No matter how many times I make the bed,
Every single morning, it needs to be done again.

No matter how neat and organized the house is
when I leave my husband watching the kids,
I always come home to find a mountain of clutter.

No matter how often I clean the sliding glass door,
It's just a matter of minutes until nose and fingerprints appear.

No matter how many dishes are washed after dinner,
There magically appear a sink full before I go to bed.

No matter how many times I go to the supermarket,
My kids still open the refrigerator door with the complaint,
"There's nothing to eat!"

And how many loads of laundry will it take
To get me into Heaven?

Susan Rogers Norton

Reflections

Going Home

Come fly the winds of memory
Beyond the clouds of time,
To frolic in the fields of youth
And search for peaks to climb.

Love flourishes forever,
The skies are endless blue;
Believing is the magic
That makes our dreams come true.

Age may slow the mortal pulse
And losses make us cry
But home is just a prayer away—
God gives us wings to fly.

C. David Hay

Reflections

A Sweet Tradition

The day we moved into this house
grandmother presented me
with a small gold box filled with fine sugar;
a symbol for the sweetness that transforms
a house into a home.

On the day my daughters
move away on their own, I will separate
the granules from the gold box, to share
all the sweetness that is yet to come.

Susan Fridkin

Reflections

Like a Statue

Like a statue, I remain motionless,
my window seat allows me to be
a silent spectator. How delightful!

It's like looking into a large aviary
where creatures stay, safe from
predators and harmful elements.

They hop from limb to limb
in search of nits, gnats, and tiny bugs
to fill their miniature puffed-up bodies.

Only my eyes move . . . watching,
breathing quietly so as not to alert them
that I am right here next to them.

Sitting this close, I wonder,
"Who's inside the aviary,
the birds or me?"

Mary Lenore Quigley

Sweet Summer Night

Holding a stick with a marshmallow crown
over the barbeque fire, toasting brown.
Graham crackers and chocolate bars
making s'mores under the stars.

Sandra Holmes McGarrity

Reflections

Marks of a True Home

The slightly worn floorboards
recall each baby cooing in the rocker.
Faint notches on the door frame
remember our children's growing years.
A stand of trees, old and new,
cherish every anniversary.

With our memories,
we have marked this place
as our one true home.

Nancy Priff

Reflections

A Place Remembered

In the shadows of our mind
Lives a place of long ago
That time will never change
Because we loved it so.

The country lane less travel worn,
The house all trimmed in white,
Twilight song of peepers
On a tranquil summer's night.

The flowers bloomed eternal
With a sky of endless blue;
It was a piece of heaven
Where all our dreams came true.

Visions of our loved ones,
They live and always will—
For no one ever dies in
The place that time stands still.

It was a perfect sanctum
From where we left to roam;
A hideaway of yesterday—
Our hearts still call it home.

C. David Hay

Reflections

The First Thought

In the dawning moments
of each day
my heart
fills with gratitude:
thank you
for my space.

Joan Noëldechen

In the Spring, She

watches the women mowing lawns,
trimming hedges, clearing debris from their fences;
envies those painting shutters, changing storm
windows, scattering new grass seed, watering.
She reads the real estate listings for houses
with character, property with quirks, old churches,
large barns, Victorians with odd shaped rooms,
tiny cottages with screened in porches, windows
wall to wall, wondering at their history, the people
whose lives they held. Once on a visit to Ohio,
she ran her hand over the rough foundation wall
of the Kirkland Temple, bits of broken crockery still
visible in the mortar, admiring the women who made
the long trek west and sacrificed their cherished china
for the need to put down roots. The Woman comes
from women who made do with carefully
pieced quilts, rag rugs, furniture thickly painted
from discarded cans; women who worked
as bowling pin setters to feed their families;

her great-great-aunt's hair still hanging behind glass,
braided and twisted into flowers after her death.
The Woman is good at making nests, remaking spaces,
shaking new life into the old, worn pieces onto a whole,
but she wonders if she will ever own a place, land
she can dig a garden into, pull weeds from, watch
the things she loves take root and hold.
She dreams of a geodesic dome surrounded
by wildflowers with a maze of climbing structures
and decks, "Funny Farm" etched in stone at the gate.
She desires to grow old and crotchety there, brown
as a raisin, slamming her walking stick against the wall
when irritated, singing with lusty lungs, continuing
to discover herself within words until the day she dies.

Nita Penfold

We Shape Our Buildings

We shape our buildings and then they shape us.

Winston Churchill
(1874–1965)

A Safe Place

Cherished home,
its pillars and floors,
keep all safe
behind its doors.
Grace the rooms
with peace and love;
let windows pour
in light from above.
On our porch
amid soft speech,
friends find rest
God within reach.

Judy Barnes

Reflections

If There Is Righteousness

If there is righteousness in
the heart there will be
beauty in the character.
If there be beauty in the
character, there will be
harmony in the house.
If there is harmony in the
home, there will be order in
the nation. When there is
order in the nation, there
will be peace in the world.

Confucius
(551–479 BC)

Reflections

Home is Oneness

Home is oneness, home is my original nature. It is right here, simply in what is. There is nowhere else I have to go, and nothing else I have to become.

Tony Parsons

Author Index

Permissions & Acknowledgments

Grateful acknowledgment is made to the authors and publishers for the use of the following material. Every effort has been made to contact original sources. If notified, the publisher will be pleased to rectify an omission in future editions.

Judy Barnes for "Housewarming" and "A Safe Place."

Gwyneth M. Bledsoe for "Aromatic Memories" and "Live Well Within Your New Home."

Mary Huff Chandler for "A Feeling of Home."

Cindy Chuksudoon for "A Prayer for Our Home" and "Hearts at Home."

Jennifer Lynn Clay for "Paradise."

Elayne Clift for "Now and Then."

SuzAnne C. Cole for "Farewell to Our Home."

Barbara Crooker for "Turning the Garden Under," and "All Week Long, the Irises Have Unfolded,."

Corrine De Winter for "No Matter What Happens," "We Pray This House," and "An Evening Grace."

Mary Katherine Devine for "Memories."

Annie Dougherty for "Hand and Hand—Heart to Heart."

Dena Dyer for "We Give Thanks Through the Seasons."

Julia Taylor Ebel for "Mountain Retreat" and "In a Garden."

Lori Eberhardy for "Little Souls" and "For Our Anniversary."

Malinda Fillingim for "The Joy of Belonging."

Anne Calodich Fone for "Our Hearts" and "Heart-light."

Sheila Forsyth for "On Entering a New Home."

Susan Fridkin for "A Sweet Tradition."

Marilyn Huntman Giese for "Moving-In-Day Prayer."

Ingrid Goff-Maidoff for "House Blessing," excerpted from *Good Mother, Welcome* by Ingrid Goff-Maidoff, published by Sarah's Circle Publishing. Copyright © 1994 by Ingrid Goff-Maidoff. Reprinted by kind permission of Ingrid Goff-Maidoff.

C. David Hay for "Christmas Past," "Going Home," and "A Place Remembered."

Barbara J. Holt for "In Celebration of a Newborn."

Sharon Hudnell for "Cabin Prayer."

The Reverend Gary W. Huffman for "In Appreciation of the Family Pet," "A Morning Grace for Family," "Happy Birthday to You," "Family Reunion Grace," and "Thanksgiving Grace" by Margaret Anne Huffman.

The Reverend J. Lynn James for "A Ritual for Moving."

Joanne Keaton for "Home Song."

Arlene Gay Levine for "Crossing the Threshold."

Andrea L. Mack for "More Than a House" and "Today Is Yours."

Carol L. MacKay for "An RV Blessing."

Sandra E. McBride for "Bless This Beloved Old Farmhouse" and "Letting Go."

Sandra Holmes McGarrity for "Blessing for a Retirement Home" and "Sweet Summer Night."

Carol Murray for "A Toast."

Shirley Nelson for "On Leaving My Special Place" and "Bless This Garden."

Kent Nerburn for "A Ceremony of the Ordinary," excerpted from *Small Graces* by Kent Nerburn, published by New World Library. Copyright © 1998 by Kent Nerburn. Reprinted by kind permission of Kent Nerburn.

Joan Noëldechen for "The First Thought."

Susan Rogers Norton for "The Infinity of Housework" and "My Garden in a Box."

Nita Penfold for "In the Spring, She."

Nancy Priff for "More Than Bricks and Wood" and "Marks of a True Home."

Mary Lenore Quigley for "I Walk with You" and "Like a Statue."

Linda Goodman Robiner for "The Enlargement of Time."

Kate Robinson for "Our Hands Were Moved."

Marjorie Rommel for "Blessing for a New House."

Andria W. Rosenbaum for "Blessing for a Jewish Home."

Gwen Tremain Runyard for "To My Children."

Linda Lee Ruzicka for "Night Blooming Garden."

Mary Kolada Scott for "Housewarming Blessing."

Joanne Seltzer for "To Life."

Rabbi Rami M. Shapiro for "We Give Thanks."

Molly Srode for "Morning's Gift."

Paula Timpson for "A Child's Sandcastle."

Donna Wahlert for "My Grandmother's Kitchen."

Louise I. Webster for "Christmas Eve Grace."

Jill Williams for "Each Chanukah Candle."

Norma Woodbridge for "Gratitude" and "Prayer in Community."

Rebecca K. Wyss for "Our Children Are Like Seeds."

About the Author

June Cotner is an accomplished author, anthologist, and speaker. Her books altogether have sold more than 600,000 copies. June has appeared on national radio programs, and her books have been featured in many national publications, including *USA Today, Better Homes & Gardens, Woman's Day,* and *Family Circle.* She teaches workshops and gives presentations at bookstores throughout the country and at the Pacific Northwest Writer's Association Conference, the Pacific Northwest Booksellers Association Conference, and The Learning Annex centers in New York and California.

A graduate of the University of California at Berkeley, June is the mother of two grown children and lives in Poulsbo, Washington, with her husband, two dogs, and two cats. Her hobbies include yoga, hiking, and cross-country skiing.

For more information, please visit June's web site at www.junecotner.com.